Walking Home

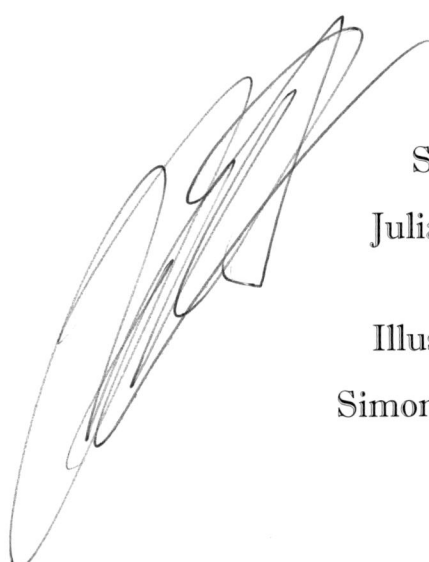

Stories by
Julian M. Miles

Illustrations by
Simon J. Mitchener

ISBN 978-0-9932873-2-9
9 780993 287329 >

The original version of 'If You Go Down to the Woods' appears in the Destinies *anthology, along with 'Stationary' and '262'. Stowaway' and 'Forever Song' are from* Tangents, *while 'Lesson of the Snows' first appeared in* Come Tomorrow.

Leyshai and Grish star in the novel Stalking Time, *which is currently in progress. However, 'Old Masters' and 'Relix' are unique to this book.*

Text, design and layout by Julian M. Miles.
Original cover and all interior art (except Lizards of the Host items) by Simon J. Mitchener. All rights reserved.

Photograph of Julian M. Miles by Maricel Dragan.
Printed and bound in the UK by Inky Little Fingers.

Inner rear cover: Original art by Simon J. Mitchener, except for: Fire in Mind by Carl Critchlow. The Borsen Incursion by Genji Lim. Come Tomorrow and Daughter of Eons by Tina LC. Long Way Home by Ian TP. Stars of Black (King in Yellow) by Joe Broers. This Mortal Dance, Winter Magic, Single White Male and Stars of Black (yellow star) by Julian M. Miles. All rights reserved.

Visit us online:
Lizards of the Host Publishing: www.lothp.co.uk
Julian M. Miles (a.k.a. Jae): www.lizardsofthehost.co.uk
Simon J. Mitchener: simonjm.devianart.com
Maricel Dragan: www.slitsight.com
Inky Little Fingers: www.inkylittlefingers.co.uk
Joe Broers: zombiequadrille.deviantart.com
Carl Critchlow: www.carlcrtichlow.com
Tina LC: tlcdigitalart.deviantart.com
Genji Lim: genjjilim.deviantart.com
Ian TP: iantp.deviantart.com

DEVILISH

I WON'T BITE

For all who enthuse about my stories and cover art.
And those who encourage Simon to keep creating.

Without you lot, this would be much less fun.
Thank you.

Another Morning

Another morning, another hangover, another tree.

Every time I go out these days, I end up paralytic and convinced of the need to rest on high ground. Urban warfare does that to you, along with flatlining your circle of friends and getting you acquainted with the local police. On first name terms, in my case. At least nobody got hospitalised this time – I'm in a tree, not in a cell.

A 'large' noise on my six makes me start. Something big just moved. Really big. I'm just contemplating staying still when the big thing sneezes like an A10 letting rip. What the bloody hell sneezes like that? And what replies in a language that sounds like a cat being drowned in a water-butt?

I roll over carefully and freeze. Just like the 'be a rock' my instructor drilled into me, except this is paralysis, not choice.

That's a dragon with a saddle and barding, and a cat-headed amazon standing with an arm on its flank, like it's what she does every morning! Maybe she does. But not around here.

Last night must have been a serious bender, because the residual alcohol is still damping my emotions. Otherwise I'd be doing a poor imitation of an Olympic sprinter while making a likely-to-be-futile attempt at escape.

She's looking my way. Oh, not good.

It's looking my way as well. Oh, crap.

"William Regnares of the Seventy-Fifth?"

The accent is almost Somalian, but crisper on the sibilants. I nod.

"Clive Nugleat sent me."

That's not possible. Clive got vapourised, three years ago, in a nameless Iraqi compound.

She sees me shaking my head: "He told me to tell you 'I will never leave a stricken comrade'."

I cannot help myself. The words come unbidden: "To fall into the hands of the enemy."

The dragon nods and growls at the cat-woman. She nods: "Clive did not die. The queen's sorceress plucked him from certain death to aid us. He is a deadly soldier. The 'rangers' he trained are leaderless now that he has been captured. He always said that his men and women could rescue him, but they would need leading by someone from the Seventy-Fifth. You were his choice."

I have a shaking fit, which moves me smoothly from tree to ground, without preparation. As I lie there, trying to get air into my lungs, she intrudes on my view of branches and sky.

"You smell like a warrior lost in the peace after war. Clive said you would become like him."

So that's why Clive re-upped.

Her smile reveals a lot of silver-white teeth. "My queen offers a life of danger and excess. You will fight things beyond your present comprehension and enjoy rewards beyond your wildest dreams."

I grin. This one I know. "I have very wild dreams, lady."

The head of the dragon pushes her out of the way. The brown eyes start to glow. "Then you better come and see if we can meet the ticket, Ranger."

Oh, that was slick. I've been played.

"I'll come. Just so I can tell Clive he's a bastard to his face."

Another morning, another hangover, another world. Much better.

Glimpse

Serenya loved cutting through the old quarter on a sunny day. Something about the bright light and variable shadows allowed her to imagine when this place had been a market, its previous inhabitants scurrying about under the banners that had been tied back to allow stallholders to hawk their wares. When real fires burned in the hanging sconces as night fell.

This place had been a market for centuries, right up to the Renaissance of Earth, when it had been restored to its former state. While she appreciated the goals of the 'Great Renaissance', she thought that the bustling life characterised by some form of period market would have been a better purpose. Show off life, not empty halls and courtyards with beautiful hangings.

Before being a market, the place had been some sort of devotional haven for a military order, apparently inspired by the sighting of an angel within this very building, or so legend told. Prior to that, it had been a noble's residence from the moment it had stopped being a farmer's field.

She'd forgotten her hydro. The sun was beating down, turning her view monochrome under its harsh light. Something flickered at the corner of her eye. She slowed her step, hand rising to where a fly caught her hair. As she freed the insect, the flickering of her vision started to concern her.

The stuttering of her vision ended with a blink that didn't involve her eyelids. Glancing ahead, she saw one of the costumed tour guides, obviously startled by her presence. With a smile at him, she continued her walk, noting that by the time she passed the alcove he'd stepped back into, he'd gone about his duties.

*

It was in my fourteenth year that I was assigned the privilege of guarding the banner yard. The duty carried no danger, as the yard was deserted except upon high days and holy days, but to be given the duty of watching there was a sign of favour.

I had done the seneschal that favour by rousting the squire who had accosted his daughters, and he, in turn, had mentioned my name to the Duke. How little did I know of God's subtle hand, then.

So I stood in the shadows at the edge of the yard as the sun rose high and noon passed. Blinking my eyes to clear sweat from them, I was determined to stand firm, without retreat to the cooler depths of the alcoves. After all, the Duke could come by at any time. I had to be seen. Had I known that my task that day was to see, not be seen, I might have saved myself considerable discomfort.

I had stood my post since lauds, and as the fabled heat of the afternoon intensified, I found myself blinking more than I was looking, if truth be told. It was as I opened my eyes wide in an attempt to trickle the sweat away that the yard turned to black and white under the sun's leeching glare. Dazzled by a flash of reflected glory, I dropped my gaze and when I looked up, she stood in the yard. My breath caught. Her flaxen hair lay in braided queues, and she dressed with less modesty than some ruttish wench at the tavern, yet her air of serenity belied such cheap environs. Somehow, I knew she was a man-of-arms, for all that that pursuit be inappropriate for a woman. And with that errant prescience, a certainty came upon me: a warrior angel honoured the banner yard, appearing to me, sixth son of no mark, to show that the Lord's grace could extend even to one as lowly as myself, were I but to take his directive from her presence.

Oh glory! At my realisation, she smiled, and my heart skipped like it would spring from my breast and ascend upon her trail. Then, her mercy bestowed, in a blink of God's eye, she was gone.

That very day I swore myself to His service, and soon found those who took my vision to heart, founding the Order of Cardiel, after she who had appeared before me.

To this day, I have striven to be worthy of His grace via her mercies, defending those who would rise from wretched station against them that would preserve the status quo in defiance of His teachings. Until my dying day, where, God willing, I will meet my saving grace once again, I serve with heart, soul and sword.

Gilles George Lavarde,
Grand Master by the Grace of God,
Order of Cardiel.

CHAPEL OF CARDIEL

Coming Home

The stars are always prettier on the way back in. Watching that sparkling void always sets my mind to drifting.

We used to laugh about 'going out to infinity', making our way across the vastness, scavenging what we needed as we got further from mankind. To see a place no-one else has seen before, and which could remain unseen after our visit. The only change would be a little beacon to let people know that this place was recorded in the Grand Atlas.

Ancient mariners used to refer to a 'siren song'. Explorers of the benthic deeps reported an elusive behemoth, always at the edge of their sensors. The first space missions reported a whole range of things. After you sorted through the maladies induced by being a human in a tin can hurtling across the big empty, you got two common themes: faces at the viewports and songs in your head.

I've seen the watchers at my portals. They used to scare me. Now I talk to them like old friends, and I swear that their expressions have softened. Their songs may be in my head, but ever since that crash as a lad, I've always had songs going on in my head. Made me a bit strange. Made me remote. Made me ideal for deep space.

Six of us set off, the usual balance of sexes: four women and two men. Over the next twelve years, we just about exhausted the combinations of love and hate. But the balance we found died with Timo. I can still see his shocked face now, looking down at the hole where his heart should have been. A micro meteor got Laney as well, except hers went through hydroponics too. That gave us weeks of strange rations and a lack of trace stuff that I still blame Charley's madness on. She'd been odd from get go, but after the rationing she turned murderous. The day she turned on Alicia, I was in the cabin next door. By the time I'd kicked their door in, Alicia was dead and Charley was coughing her last. Alicia and I had been on and off since we left Mars. I didn't try to save her killer. Kinsela shouted at me a lot about that, but calmed down as her guilt eased: becoming Charley's warders for the rest of our natural lives didn't appeal to her, either.

After that, Kinsela and I spent eight comfortable years sleeping through skip-jumps and distributing beacons with glee, sending data spears back, sure we had the best find rate of all the expeditions.

She died as we left Arcadia VII, a malfunctioning data spear turning her into a pair of drifting legs and an expanding sphere of glowing dust. I reset the data, named the planet after her, cut a new packet, sent a second - carefully checked - data spear on its way, then got the heck out of there.

Next system, I retrieved a data spear. The despatch date was a decade before. Said the Outer Reach Expeditions were over, that we were the last crew still out in the long night.

As I brought the tug back to the ship, I stared out of a side portal and saw a watcher with Alicia's face. I swear she looked at the data packet racked next to me and shook her head.

I kept going. Didn't acknowledge, just sent spears back from every viable world, tracing a dotted trail into the unknown. When I ran out of beacons, nine years back, I cut up a spear and sealed a data packet into the disc I made, then set that in the correct orbit for a beacon. A duplicate data pack got sent back.

I'm coming back from sending my last spear. The spotlights shine on the scoured side of the *Chunshun*, picking highlights from the welcoming black depths of the tug bay. I haven't seen Alicia, or anyone else, at my portals on this trip, but I think that's because I already know what she wants.

We're going to keep going, my ghosts and I. Going to keep going until I join them.

Stationary

He glanced up at the sky and sighed into his facemask. Mid-altitude rain clouds that would become a complete overcast within twenty minutes. Chance of precipitation rising by five percent for every ten minute increment after that. He had twenty-five minutes at best. Rain meant he had to retreat and would pay the price for failure. Which was just not an option. The last time had resulted in a week of hell.

Focus. A single tree with a primitive child's entertainment construct on the one load-bearing branch. As the device was not moving, the branch above was probably clear. The presence of small indigenous wildlife in the foliage above raised the chance to near-certainty.

Scattered shrubbery to the left was too open to permit concealment within active ranges. The long grasses beyond the tree and to the right of it were his target zones. If pressed, he would bet on the long grass beyond the tree, but guesswork was only a ticket to losing this. He had scoured this side and he was convinced that his perimeter was secure. No chance of the target sneaking back into areas he had already checked: the reason for his failure last time. He winced again as memories of the subsequent week distracted him.

Focus. He had a single target. The other three were dealt with. They just were not as good as this one, a veteran in evasion and subterfuge. This was the problem. Such an expert would anticipate his scrutiny and actions.

He smiled as he remembered his instructor's counsel many years before: "If you know he's expecting you or is better than you at what you're attempting, take his advantage away. Move the game to a place where you have the edge."

He hung his head momentarily. Of course. He stood up and strode forward, placing himself in the perfect sentry position for the area around the tree. He relaxed into a stance he could hold - and had, on previous occasions - for hours. Then he dropped himself into the light trance of watchfulness and waited.

The long grass barely moved, but his trance-induced spatial hyper-awareness spotted it. He pointed his assault rifle at the slight disturbance in the grass and shouted: "Zott!"

The small figure stood up and placed its hands on its hips.

"Not fair, Mister Bruin. You used your sensors."

Captain of the Guard Devan Bruin shook his head in despair. Now for an hour of "No I didn't", "Oh yes you did". But at least a week of Danburg Junior noisily counting coup at every opportunity had been avoided.

Dis-Joint Custody

Gillian eased her grip on the Heckler and Koch MP5K-PDW. She had paid extra for the assault magazines and suppressor, but regretted the weight now. It was a superb weapon but the need to carry it one-handed while herding her kids had not been part of the tactical considerations. Then again, the two-tone suede Louboutin shoes with four-inch heels were hardly suitable footwear for any firefight outside of a film set.

Beyond the door to the first floor, the sounds of mayhem and confusion continued to diminish as the gunfire became sporadic. The last thing that Jeff had expected was for her to slam into his secured luxury apartment block – fetchingly situated off Wenceslas Square in Prague - with all guns blazing and a six-man fireteam at her back.

"Ruby, this is Wideboy. The locals have called for fire support. We have Hinds and Pandurs inbound." This ear-wrap comms unit was superb. She must remember to recommend it to Major Thomas; her old crew would love it.

"Bricky, this is Ruby. Drop the bridge before they reach it."

"Can't I even put a couple of 'em in the drink?"

"Bricky, we're here to get my kids, not to start a war with the Czech Republic."

"Just thinking of future employment opportunities, boss."

She grinned and rested the suppressor of the H&K on the stair rail. "After this, I don't think Eastern Europe will be featuring on our itinerary for a while."

"Good point boss. You always did have a touch for strategy."

"Bricky, this is Killeye. Stop being an arse."

Gillian chuckled. Her big brother couldn't stop defending her, even when she was commander and he was sniper.

"Killeye, what's the view?"

"The building won't be surrounded until the army turn up. Until then, a blacked-up Sarath won't attract notice for being in the wrong place with the wrong insignia."

She leaned forward and looked down at her kids. Malc looked scared; Anna was concentrating on reassuring him as a way to counter her own fear.

"Hey, you two."

They both looked up, faces lighting with hope.

"Fancy a ride in a tank?"

The Sarath wasn't actually a tank, but it would qualify. It wasn't even a Sarath, really. That was the Indian version. But calling it a BVP-2V didn't come easily off the tongue in situations like this.

"Is that so Dad's gang can't get us?" Malc always had the downside view. Anna had the upside. But in this case, glossing the details wouldn't help. She nodded.

Malc smiled. The absolute trust in his indestructible Mum nearly broke Gillian's control. Not now. She could blubber and wail later. She had a clean getaway to make first.

"Ruby, this is Knockdown. All the goons are down, hiding or running. Everybody wants us to play nice all of a sudden."

"That's because you look like something out of the online wargames they play, but kill for keeps."

"Why thank you, boss."

"Ruby, this is Razor. Don't encourage him."

"Razor, he's your problem, woman. Haven't you housetrained him yet?"

Gillian heard the thump of Razor punching Knockdown in his football-sized shoulder.

"Setting my woman on me boss? That's low."

"Talk to my ex about that."

Knockdown and Razor stole glances back at the bullet-riddled and smoking remains of Jeff Kzejpik's lounge. Somewhere in the ruins ex-husband, ex-crimelord Jeff lay with a look of fatal surprise on his bloodied face and at least twenty parabellum slugs in his torso.

"Roger that, boss."

"Now the niceties are concluded, let's go home. Killeye, let our ride know we're coming. How long to exit the Sarath and get on the whirlybird?"

She could hear the satisfaction in her brother's voice. "We don't. We just drive in and it goes. I got us a Halo."

The largest production helicopter ever built should do for a ride home, but – "It makes a big target, Killeye."

"Did I forget to mention the Havoc I hired as escort? Happy birthday, sis."

As cheers and laughter sounded over the comm. Gillian looked down at her kids again.

"Time to go home. In a tank-carrying helicopter."

Malc looked up. "No way!"

She smiled. "No lie. Chris got it for my birthday."

Anna stood up and smiled at her mum. "You have the best brother ever. Malc's gotta try harder."

Malc looked serious for a moment. "Give me time, Anna. I'll never let you down."

Gillian felt an icy chill of premonition. Another brother dedicated to his sister's wellbeing at the expense of himself? She'd have to diffuse that. Not totally, just enough to allow him independence.

"All units, bail for transport by the east fire exit."

Everyone acknowledged. She straightened from her ready position, shouldered the H&K and picked up the shoes. Sally at the hairdressers would kill her if she left them behind.

- ON THE BACK COVER -

The Last Shuttle

The sole remaining Tower of Dawning Sorrow will fall, fittingly, at dawn tomorrow.

Across frozen ranges, the scream of the shuttle's deceleration echoes, a noise fit to wake the dead. It fades without raising so much as a gust of wind. All it achieves is the momentary shattering of a silence so profound it is entrancing.

This world 'died' so long ago Earth had only aquatic inhabitants at the time. We don't even know what the residents of this place looked like: they expunged all record of themselves before slipping softly into extinction, or journeying off into the depths of space.

I'm sure they didn't erase themselves as thoroughly as some of my colleagues claim. It's simply the passage of a vast gulf of time that's finished what the Limuin started. Sadly, the cause - be it guilt or ennui - is one of the losses.

All we are sure of is the evocative names, left on glorious maps made by fusing gemstones into slabs of bedrock. The Pinnacles of Chean used to reflect the light of the sun, but now only hills and an upland desert mark where they once stood. What great sorrow necessitated the row of Towers along the coast of this continent, we shall never know. The Skiffhavens of Yerewn are like gigantic, time-smoothed crenellations lain on their side. They stretch for a hundred kilometres, and each bay is bigger than the ship that my shuttle will take me to. A Limuin skiff must have been a thing of wonder to behold. I simply cannot envision what a fleet of them would have looked like.

The names and the maps have been scanned and recorded. Doomed Limua and its appellations have caught the imaginations of everyone, even those who considered themselves jaded. And where interest is generated, livelihoods are made: writers plot feverishly and singers compose in a mix of fervour and awe. They have the names and titles, all that is needed is the romance and derring-do to bring lost wonders back to life.

I'm carrying the last data, as the fragment of planet that is headed this way will reduce Limua to rubble. This place doesn't warrant the efforts that would be expended to save a habited world. While there is much to be said for letting nature take its course, I am saddened to leave and already grieving over the loss to come.

We go further every day, but, while my colleagues wax lyrical about the finds yet to be made, I am sure in my heart that anything to match the haunting beauty of Limua and its enigmatic spires will never be found.

The shuttle descends into view. Time to take my last walk across the time-worn Crags of Eshilaluin to meet it, while I muse over what mankind will eventually leave behind.

Lesson of the Snows

The cave is warm and crowded. Eating is done and all present turn their eyes to the loreman when he rises to stand by the hearthfire, his shadow growing huge upon the rough-hewn wall behind him. He turns full circle to regard all, and everyone feels they are his sole listener. That is why he is the loreman. He is the bard, his memory the history of all. He alone has done the seven year walk, visiting every tribe to listen to their stories. Tonight he tells a history woven from those threads.

"Listen well and hear the lesson that the snows whisper. Our forefathers conjured demons to do their bidding. Great cities of unnatural rock spread over the land whilst our forefathers flew above in carts that challenged eagles for mastery of the skies.

They harnessed demons into constructs that provided whatever the user demanded, without the touch of crafter or smith. While the dark utopias engendered by those pitiless methods spread, our forefathers lost touch with the land. Their demon minions had removed the necessity to heed unto nature.

Time passed and in their greed they strove, tribe against tribe, in terrible battles that turned good land into the night-blue crystal lowlands, reduced forests to ash, and struck down cities with greater ease than we tear down termite mounds.

At the end, our forefathers withdrew to the mountain vastnesses, building themselves great underground palaces in which to abide until the demon taints had been quieted by weather and time. But in their fear, they set about these havens armies of demon guards to protect them. They were still so fearful of other tribes that they forgot to defend against the little ills that even our children know to protect against.

It is said that a pestilence rose amongst them and the dying was an evil thing to behold. We know that the founders of our tribes were those who fled, evading the demon guards surrounding the palaces - guards turned to merciless captors by the absence of overseers lost to disease.

In those palaces are the seeds of all that is needed to start again, to heal the blights upon the land, to calm the icy wrath of the sky.

The demon guards have outlived their masters, yet are still bound to their duty. Until they fall, we can only gaze from afar upon the sites of these hidden citadels, and despair. Our salvation is waiting, but the sins of our forefathers are not yet expiated. We must continue to survive this land of seven-moon winters until we are forgiven for the arrogance of our ancestors."

If You Go Down to the Woods

It was the Halloween ball, spun across the domain of mankind's star-spanning empire, the start of the three Home festivals kept to remind all where they came from. Couples whirled while singles eyed each other hopefully across the glitter of the free-fall dance floor, or manoeuvred for choice seats at the thronged bars and tables.

Outside the packed hangar, there was the usual mess of mechanisms and cabling that always sprung up to support such festivities. Down a side corridor beyond the gravity generators, a small group of people stood looking down, their attitude far from the festive cheer their clothing hinted at.

"Halloween and we have a death. Fitting, sad and annoying."

Sheriff Pavitch looked at Deputy Burton with disapproval: "I am so glad you nearly saved yourself by including 'sad' in that."

The humming from the silver case by the corpse stopped. Doctor Delores Regarmo stared at the results screen and then looked up with puzzlement on her face: "He's been de-oxygenated."

"What?"

The stereo response made her smile. For all their bickering, they were so alike in their effectiveness at finding criminals. She pointed at the corpse's blue lips and dark hollows under his eyes, then lifted his hand to show blue fingers.

"Cyanosis is only the start of it. There's no oxy- in his haemoglobin and his lungs would be better used as soles for shoes: completely flat."

The Marshalls looked at each other. Pavitch smiled at Burton: "Okay, instant karma for you objecting to being taken from your partying."

"Thanks. I take it that this is unusual?"

"Unheard of, more like. Never seen it and no record on the database here or on the main one over at Riordan Station."

Burton looked up at the ceiling ducts: "Great. I had just found me a green-headed woman, and suddenly I have no time."

Delores paused and unwound something from the victim's finger: "Your green-haired lady. She has a beautiful head of hair, about forty centimetres long, and sports a clear lip shine?"

Burton stared at her and nodded. Delores held up a long strand of green hair and pointed to the gloss patches on the victim's lips.

"Then you and he shared an interest. If she wasn't the last person to see this chap alive, she was the second to last by only a few minutes."

Pavitch and Burton headed back to the ballroom. They decided quickly that they wouldn't ruin anyone else's Halloween by calling in until they had a definite target. Jerome Wilkins was dead and while he needed justice done, many hands would generate nothing except perturbation. An hour later they had finished scanning the ballroom and pulled up all the footage of the opening parade. They found Jerome looking lonely in the parade, but smiling happily later, dancing with a very attractive green-haired woman. Burton swore when he saw her, distracting Pavitch from the faint glimmer of something at the back of his memory.

"Said her name was Eva. Had a funny accent. Damn but my luck is off."

Pavitch laughed: "Instant karma."

Burton said something scathingly un-festive and stormed off to get more coffee. Pavitch turned back to the console and started doing the forms that would be required regardless of the outcome.

The radial corridor curved gradually, something that you started to notice more the longer you were on the station. Short-term visitors benefitted from the perspective-straightening paintwork, while it only irritated long serving personnel. Burton stood at the machine, idly drumming his fingers as he waited for it to put together the blasphemy to coffee purists that Pavitch drank. He was just wondering if he would ever get a break on the romantic front like Pavitch had, marrying a gorgeous stripper from Feldane - who happened to be a graduate down on her luck - when a touch on his shoulder made him grunt in surprise. He looked around to have his gaze caught by a pair of the greenest eyes.

"Hello Gareth. I missed you. Something I said?"

She was barely a hand span from him, hair moving lazily. Her dress of gossamer silks shaded in earth tones revealed suggestive details that made him swallow before answering.

"Hello Eva. Sorry about that, but I see you got side-tracked too. Want to tell me about Jerome?"

Her eyes went wide and her lip trembled. Tears welled up: "What happen to him? Is he alright? He left in a hurry after a man, I worry but he told me not to tell until later."

Burton relented. The concern in those eyes actually made the hairs on his arms rise. He leaned back on the vending machine.

"Who is he to you?"

"He looks out for me. When I arrive in 'ponics, he made sure I got no trouble. I thought he was after my body. But he wasn't. He cared."

Burton nodded. Most of the folk on Allegheny Station were good folk. He and Pavitch were here for times like this, when a bad apple bobbed to the surface.

"The man. What did he look like?"

"I know him; he works the sludge pits in 'ponics. Jerome looks after the gardens so he has to make sure the sludge is just right for the plants in the garden."

Allegheny Gardens were frequently described as a marvel of human dedication. The huge, multi-tiered hanging gardens had been started by the second Commodore. He'd had an idea to give people a place to relax where they couldn't see metal walls no matter where they looked. It had worked, although the skills required to maintain such a verdant space so many million miles from Earth had left it as a singular testament to those who maintained it with love and pride. Since Earth had suffered the Second Blight, some of the specimens in Allegheny Gardens were the only examples of their kind remaining.

Burton decided not to upset Eva with the news of her protector's death just yet.

"Was the man in festival dress?"

"No, was in overalls."

Burton checked his chrono. Pavitch would be doing the paperwork for a while yet.

"Let's go and see if the man Jerome followed is back on duty."

They headed down to the hydroponics section, situated above the core as the planet-like spectrum of emissions seemed to help the growth. It was dimly lit and humid. A night-time jungle of frames supporting the greenery that sustained so much. They trekked through the long room until they came to an open door next to a warning sign stating 'Keep Closed'. Burton nodded. He liked it when clues were obvious. He pointed to it, then leant close to Eva's ear so he could whisper: "No-one on this station would leave a door open contrary to warnings. Looks like our man is a little light on reading skills. Where does this lead?"

She turned her head quickly, and for a moment and their lips touched. Burton jerked his head back with a mumbled apology. She smiled, eyes sparkling in the dim light: "It's 'ponics access to the gardens."

They moved carefully down the corridor after closing the door. At the end, they passed through three atmosphere screens before coming out into a section of the gardens that Burton had never seen. It had been set up as a tranquil woodland pool, overhung with various twisted branches from which moss dangled almost to the water in places. The whole thing seemed to be designed to draw attention to the willow tree that stood on the far side. Burton looked about before gesturing around: "I've never seen this section. Where is it from?"

Eva smiled: "Russian woodland. Over there is tree I look after. Out from cold as ground is good now."

Burton straightened up. He looked back and down at Eva before extending his hand: "Looks like we're going to get a closer look, the trail goes that way."

Taking his hand, she accompanied him into the shaded growth.

The air around the pool was cool and the moss under the willow was spread like a deep-pile carpet of palest emerald. Eva sat down and put her back against the willow: "Can we stop? I want to know about Jerome."

Burton hated this bit. A good woman reduced to a lump of raw emotion by the actions of a bad man. He told her as gently as he could, but as her face went white and her hands clenched his in a near-excruciating grip, he knew this was going to be grim. Tears almost spurted from her eyes as her head fell, the glorious green tresses falling to hide her expression as sobs wracked her body. Burton looked about, despite knowing they were alone, before placing an arm around her shaking shoulders. He whispered comforting nonsense until her head rose again. She lifted a hesitant hand to brush back her hair before touching his jaw gently. Her eyes went wide as she seemed to share the attraction he felt for her. Without thought, he cradled the back of her head before drawing her to him and kissing her deeply, feeling her arms around him as his chest tightened and his vision dimmed.

Pavitch looked up from the console. Forms done and no sign of Burton. He hoped his deputy had not slid back to the festivities for a quick glass of something. Just as he decided to start his search for his absent partner in the ballroom, the talkbox chirped on his belt. He tapped his ear to accept the link: "Roman? Delores. Our dangerous lady is not on the staff of this station or Riordan. I can find no record of her arrival profile either. The DNA analyser is having one of its moments with her hair, so I'll have to wait until tomorrow, after I call a tech to fix it."

Pavitch stood quickly. A stowaway? The implications of getting an unregistered person this far out were not good. Nobody made it this far without backing, and those who would back that sort of activity did not do it out of the kindness of their hearts.

"Thanks Delores. I think it's time to ruin a lot of people's festivities."

He pressed the 'Officer Call' button and moved into the briefing room to wait for his folk to arrive.

Several hours after the end of the festival, they found Burton floating in the pool by the willow, body de-oxygenated like Jerome. Pavitch had been staring at the willow for a while when Delores called him.

"Roman. I know you've found Gareth, but can you come up to the lab immediately, please?"

Pavitch had his investigative curiosity piqued. Something in Delores' voice had been off, a tone he had not heard before. He made it to the lab deck in record time. She was standing in the corridor staring at the door to her lab. From the look on her face, Pavitch identified the emotion he'd heard in her voice: fear.

"You called?"

She pointed at the door.

"If I go back in there and what I thought I saw did not happen, I will check myself into psychiatrics immediately. If what I think is in there is actually there, I may have to do the same for you. Ready?"

Pavitch nodded as he reached for his sidearm. She placed a hand over his.

"No need."

She pressed the doorpad and entered the room before anything could give her an excuse not to. He entered cautiously, seeing nothing out of place except her stool lying on its side, under the microscope table. Next to it was a torn evidence bag. He stepped nearer. Not torn. Burst. He looked back as Delores pointed to the table top.

"It's still here. Oh damn."

The table top was empty except for a short length of plant stem. Pavitch raised an eyebrow as he turned to her. She shook her head and pressed start on the microscope display unit. On the screen he saw an incredibly magnified view of what his rudimentary experience told him could be hair of some kind. As he watched, red flashes ran the length of the sample and it started to thicken rapidly. Suddenly the playback whited-out. Delores stopped the display.

"That's when I ran, as I heard the bag tear behind me."

He looked about and then pointed to the stem on the table. Delores nodded, then stepped closer to him while approaching no nearer to the table.

"That was the strand of hair from Eva."

Pavitch wished that Burton's earlier distraction had not stopped him listening to his intuition. He stepped forward and picked up the stem. Twig, actually.

Turning to Delores, he smiled a bleak smile: "We have a rare guest. Burn this and trash the report. Jerome officially died of a bad batch of hooch, as did Deputy Burton when he found the still and was overcome by fumes. Meet me down where we found Burton. I have to get a specialist."

Delores put a hand on his chest as he started to move past her: "Specialist? Who the hell do we have on transformational morphology like this?"

Pavitch grinned: "My grandmother."

Asta Pavysczyk was known as 'Auntie Witch' to most of the station. Over a century old and showing no signs of quitting anytime soon, she had followed her favourite grandson to the stars and regretted not one moment of it. She looked up as Roman entered, raising her arms for a hug before putting them down when she saw his expression.

"What is 'up' my favourite grandson? You come into my *dacha* looking like the world is upon you."

"Gareth is dead, Gramma. I think he was taken by a Rusalka. You know what that costs me to say."

Asta looked down at her lap, then raised herself and went over to hug her grandson, her movements still spry. She stood back, holding his upper arms. There were tears in her eyes.

"I am saddened that you learn the truth of my teachings in such a hard way. But tell me quick, how has a rusalki come to the stars?"

"I will show you."

They met Dolores by the pool. As she entered, Asta clapped her hands in delight.

"Oh, this is so fine. I will spend many hours here. It is just like home."

Pavitch pointed across the water at the willow.

"Gramma, is that not a Goat Willow?"

Asta peered and, with a sharp nod, followed the trail to the moss bed around the willow after waving off their warnings with a derisive snort.

She sat down on the moss and touched the trunk of the tree.

"This is old. So old. But it has only woken recently. How is this?"

"It was in stasis until this part of the garden was ready."

Asta hung her head.

"Poor little forest sprite, torn from her home while she slept."

She pulled a pin from her shawl, pricked her finger, placed it against the bark and called out: "говорить в меня."

There was a moments silence, then from the branches above a rustling of leaves combined to form a reply:

"сожалеющий."

Delores and Elgin exchanged glances as Asta chatted with the willow for a while before taking her finger from the trunk and turning to them.

"She is a young willow rusalki. Cannot even read. When she woke she thought she had been sent down to *Podsvetie* – the underworld. She is sorry for the loss of your friend and that gardener, but she was starved. From now on, she will be able to get by on livestock. She is very puzzled because she gave them fair warning but they did not seem to care."

Roman looked at the pool.

"What kind of warning?"

"She told them she a willow."

"Burton said that she said her name was Eva."

Asta shook her head sadly: "What she said was 'ива'. It means 'willow' in old Russian."

Delores bowed her head and shed a few tears for the deputy: "Sounded like 'Eva' to me."

WAITING

262

After four centuries, mankind had reached Alpha Centauri.

Captain Donal Maclachlan had just finished shaking hands with his crew when his sensor team started making unhappy noises. Moving swiftly and assuredly, as befitted a career officer, he arrived by the consoles as the unhappiness degenerated into incredulity. Decisively, he ordered the collated feed pushed to the master holo. Then he just joined in the staring.

It hung there in space, clearly derelict, sleek lines still clear, a streamlined pod under each wing and a swastika flag on the triangular tail. Donal could even see the cracked bubble of the cockpit, and pairs of white characters worn to near-obscurity on either side of the black cross on the fuselage.

"What is that?" His words fell into the sudden silence.

His second in command, a war history buff usually given to tedious lecturing, whispered in a shaky voice: "A Messerschmitt Swallow, sir. First true combat jet fighter, used during the second global conflict of the twentieth century."

Captain Maclachlan spun to face him: "Very good, TWIC. Now what in the name of Gagarin is it doing here?"

"That, sir, is a question that will baffle mankind for a very long time."

Donal stared in loathing at the impossibility shown in the holo.

"Gentlemen, we have had our thunder well and truly stolen."

*

While earth revelled in the mystery, the door of a cluttered office slammed open, several subterranean levels below what had been the Pentagon. A very flustered old man looked up to see his bleary-eyed boss stood there shaking.

"Please tell me our respected predecessors archived the notebooks of Von Braun's nutty assistant. Looks like we've been copying the work of the wrong genius."

Stowaway

She's still down there in the flight bay. I can hear her, quietly uttering words that are not ours in a way that is neither chant nor litany. They pull music from the skeleton of the ship, teasing out their own accompaniment.

I have travelled from Magellan to Rison, chatted with hundreds of spacers from every star-faring race. My data banks have encyclopaedias of knowledge in their crystalline matrices. All of it is for nothing. She's a mystery.

When she first appeared, we thought that we'd picked up a sprite, one of the fey nomads from Lurgallon. Then Crome, our ex-marine, went down to say hello and never came back. Not a trace of him. Nothing. No energy spike, no screams, no mess. Just gone like he'd never returned to the ship before we lifted.

We locked down the bay and held a frantic discussion before contacting Albeda Field, our last port of call. The lag on comms was frustrating and her words were already filling the silences between whatever noises we made.

Jorgen went to the head. He never came back. The only clue was the override on the bay door. He even relocked it properly from the inside. Then nothing.

Albeda Field did not help. Instead of forwarding our requests for aid to the main systems, they raised a 'plague ship' flag on us.

Fantella had an idea and, working with Rubius, rejigged our comms transmitter to punch a compressed data packet toward Hostria, the nearest planet with a military base. While that was going on, Saldural the medic went down to the flight bay. Same thing: relocked the door and then was gone.

Pretty soon her words were in our dreams. We couldn't sleep; we couldn't even make conversation or watch AV to distract us. Fantella and Rubius went together, like they did in all things. Nigranto the cook went a day later.

Landuth and I sat and stared at each other, drinking neat distillate until we couldn't see, then drinking more until we passed out. Her words dragged us back.

After a week, an Albedan frigate hove into firing range and queried if we required merciful release yet. After I'd finished laughing, I told them 'no' - as Landuth looked at me, nodding the opposite, with pleading despair in his eyes.

When I went to the head, Landuth went down to the bay. I came back to the words and nothing else. Landuth had even poured the last of the distillates down the recycler. He meant me to go down too. I wouldn't. For another week I held off the daily calls for 'merciful' destruction and fought the words that gradually went from nuisance to siren call. By the end of that week I had taken to handcuffing myself to the stanchion by my bunk. I had twice woken up to find myself standing in front of the flight bay door.

This is day twenty-six. The Albedan frigate has stopped calling. It hangs there in space, waiting for the lifesigns here to vanish. I'm tapping my finger, in time to the strange calling rhythm that I can now hear in her words, when there is a flash on the sensors as a huge ship arrives. The Albedan frigate moves off at flank speed without even waiting to identify the arrival. I take a scan of the ship profile and query the databanks. Two minutes later I am informed that it is a Leomuriant capital ship. The Leos are an ancient race that rarely interact with humanity. I guess we must be like a vast crowd of screaming kids to them.

My comms lights up and a slow soprano voice says: "Go to it."

I break into hysterical laughter. The universe has finally turned on me.

The voice continues: "It will not harm you. It only wants your vessel."

That stops me. They know what she is?

"Why does she want my ship?"

"Because she cannot go home without it. Her energy is depleted, so she cannot make the vast distance home. But she will not harm anyone. She depletes her energy more to send you home before she takes your ship out of this galaxy."

"Why didn't she just ask?"

"She has been. For nearly four of your weeks."

Now I feel like an intergalactic idiot.

"What is she?"

"We have no idea. For ninety centuries her kind have sporadically appeared and done what she is doing: acquiring a ship to go home. What they do here, before that, is unknown. Where 'home' is exactly is also unknown. One of our shamans, many ancestors ago, had a brief communion with one of her kind, after we lost several ships. Since then, every space port of ours has what we call a 'longship' ready. Occasionally staff at the field become aware of strange words in the air, moments before their longship lifts. We just wave them off and set up another longship."

"So what do you call them?"

"Firechylder. From the only thing our shamans can interpret of their destination: they are returning to the 'Fire Courts'. Context incomprehensible, of course."

After that, conversation is useless. I thank the Leo, place the ship in ready mode and go down to the flight bay.

She's there, silver-grey skin surrounded by turquoise flashes of an energy field, hands before her chest with fingers interlaced. It's like she's praying, luminous eyes open but focussed elsewhere. As I enter, her hair flashes from azure to flaming strands and nebulous tentacles of fiery energy. I leave the door open and gesture to it, waving her through.

Mum nearly has a heart attack as I appear in the lounge of the family apartment on Lalludor in the Ceres Cluster, two light years from what had been my ship. She rushes towards me then stops dead, pinches her nose and points toward the fresher room.

- ON THE INNER FRONT COVER -

Turnabout

This little dip in the landscape will mark the end of this pursuit. Another heretic will fall, and I, for one, will not rue her passing after the merry dance she has led us.

I gesture for my companions to wait and stride toward her, a shamelessly underdressed young fem sitting cross-legged. The aura of the relic in her hands highlights the angles of her face and the crazed light in her eyes.

She speaks without taking her gaze from me: "A long time ago, they used to make homes of glass that were as tall as elder oaks. Our ancestors flew through the air like dragons in chariots of purest steel. Knowledge was free to all, Gens and Fems, and we were proud and fair and bowed before no gods."

I hear the shocked cries behind me. Of all the fallen mendicants, Braith had fallen hardest, electing to flee through the heart of the cavern in which the blasphemies had been found. What she had discovered during the trip had obviously hardened her resolve to die unrepentant.

Raising my voice, I try one last time: "Braith of Aberystwyth, return to the Five Ways! There is forgiveness in recantation, and a good farming life to be had! Cast away that relic of a time best forgotten. Datamancy ruined us, turning the great into fools and the masses into brutal hordes. Turn your mind from the craving for knowledge! Save yourself! Save your family!"

My trump card: her siblings. I see her eyes widen and know that my duke's decision to withhold the knowing of their survival was a good tactic.

"Which of them survive?"

"I know not their names. One gen fresh out of nursery, and two fems approaching their fertile years. You have my word they will be spared if you recant."

She straightens up, the fire in her eyes lost in shadow as her lips move and the relic starts to glow.

"What if I refuse to recant?"

"Your family line will end today."

"What if I return, and take my kin by force?"

I hear laughter behind me, but something in her tone stays my mirth.

"You would need veteran warriors, child. Or a dragon."

My bodyguard, Wills, shouts derisively: "Both! Bring what you got, witchling!"

The air goes cold and still as circles of white light emanate from her like ripples on a pond. When they touch the earth, she rises slowly, until she floats at the centre of multiple rings of power.

With a 'crack' like a great branch breaking, a five-fold trigon manifests. The halos of puissance that flank it attest to its power. There are shouts from behind me.

A giant head swings into my view, and my unwilling gaze tracks left to the adult Moordrake and the ensemble that stand before it. I see a Gandrian legionary pair, a Culsuk gladiator, an Oshi devil and a Tarnutad djinn. Neither devil nor djinn ever fare from their homes alone.

I hear her voice as I spin about to race for my steed: "This is what I 'got', cleric. Your move."

My move?

"Flee! One of us must survive to warn the duke!"

Old Masters

Through a teeming, humid jungle a predator moves with stealthy ease. He is in no danger, but practice is never wasted. Being able to move without disturbing a place so rife with biological lifeforms is a skill he rarely gets to use.

A gap in the canopy lets him see the darkening skies above: more rain. Grish smiles. Leyshai always expounded the virtues of the early explorers, who named planets, places and phenomena with a total lack of romance. He was on the planet 'Pourdown', currently enjoying the first rain-free interval in three days. An interval that had just ended, he noted as the first drops of rain spattered his grey exterior.

Ahead, the shades of green that surrounded him were darkened. He hoped it was the shadow of the place, and he hoped what he sought was still there. Moving forward, he ducked under the brobdingnagian leaf of a fern - he remembered stepping over it, last time - then sank into a crouch.

The huge step pyramid formed of black metallic blocks had been partially toppled in an antiquity that predated many races Grish knew of. What remained had resisted everything nature and sentients brought to bear, until something moved in that made the place inviolate. After a few minutes, he rose and strode over to the nearest block and tapped it lightly with a finger. Notice given, he assayed the climb to the only entrance that led to the actual interior and not a trap-laden maze.

He recalled the route faultlessly, although a couple of detours were necessary due to blocks that had shifted since his last visit. Finally, he reached the entrance to the hall at the heart of the place. Noting that it had been panelled with wrought marble in the intervening time, and had also sprouted columns supporting the roof, he leant on a wall and watched the Timeless Master at his art.

An arms-breadth from the centre of the hall, a skeletal metal figure stood motionless, katana held in a two-handed grip. Not even the tassels hanging from his woven steel 'storm hat' moved. Grish waited. Nothing was so urgent as to be worthy of disturbing this tableau.

With a movement Grish had to replay to see, the figure executed a flawless upward strike, the blade seeming to fall like a leaf before sweeping upward at a speed that even other android masters could only dream of attaining. The short, arcing strike completed, the figure returned to its starting position.

Grish pushed himself off the wall: "Nice hat."

The head turned a little. Red-dot eyes regarded the shadow in which he stood. Nothing else moved.

"Only one visitor would open with that. I heard you a kilometre away, Grish Noman. Now step into the light."

Grish moved forward until a ray of watery sunlight fell on him: "Contrast filters wearing down?"

The figure moved with breath-taking speed across the hall. With a flourish, it sheathed the katana in an aged scabbard, placing it down with care.

"That would be polite."

"And if I were not to be polite, Teotan Droon?"

"Then you would say the Timeless Master is as good as blind. I have to hear my targets."

Grish looked down at the floor. Four small insects lay there, each cut into two pieces.

"I would say it has not affected your art."

"Look again."

Grish ran his opticals up to a higher magnification: "They are sliced in twain, either ahead or behind their wing roots."

"You have the truth. I have not performed a bisection from between the eyes to the tip of the tail for decades, and I had not perfected it anyway."

"You are the Timeless Master. You are the last undroid of your line, and your progenitors have been extinct for millennia. To be blunt, you are the oldest sentient I can call a friend. That you cannot continue the art you have held in trust for so long must be a loss of staggering proportions."

Droon sank into a cross-legged pose: "That is why I sent for you. I heard legends about your kind for centuries before I met you. The Undroids of the Jhangshryn, bogey-beings to scare each new generations of androids. Then, out of nowhere, you came to my jungle with that Ruinchild, and asked me to teach her. When I asked your reasons, you said she had to be nigh-on unstoppable to survive accompanying you, and my art was what would give her that edge."

Grish nodded: "And in return, I offered a favour of me, no matter what, no matter when."

Droon shrugged: "I find myself undergoing a subtle failing, that creeps upon me in gradual encroachments that take from me more than I notice, until something masterful suddenly lies outside my capability. While Leyshai trained, you alluded to certain things, things I have pondered on. It is from those things I would draw for my favour."

Grish grimaced. Long ago, he had healed Leyshai and inadvertently augmented her in the process. It was something she could never know, for it would wreak havoc upon the fragile balance she had struck with her past. Now he was being asked to spread his progenitors' dangerous gift deliberately. He paused. Leyshai was under his protection. Droon was quite capable of protecting himself.

"You want the silver mist. Be aware that it remains faithful to the Jhangshryn, and should their extinction be anything less than total, you will be beholden."

"Then my favour is twofold. First, the healing. Second, a rescue, should it become necessary. Because you are not beholden, are you?"

Grish looked at the ancient swordmaster. Once again, the millennial intuition of an artificial sentience dumbfounded him.

"I am not. Ask no more of it, and we shall proceed."

"Answer me one other thing, then."

"What?"

"Has Leyshai finally taken up the sword I gifted her?"

Grish laughed: "She has it, and I catch her practicing with it occasionally. It is a beautiful thing to behold. So beautiful, she says, that she will not sully it with combat. Her hatchets remain her preferred weapons."

Droon grunted: "Pah! Wood-chopping primitives, the lot of them."

"They are that. Somewhere in their love of fire is a truth we lack. One day I will fathom it."

"You are too much a vagabond wanderer to be a philosopher, my friend."

"Is that a privilege reserved for masters in temples, then?"

"Not at all. It gives me chills to realise how you have become so like the wandering masters of my progenitor's ancestral home."

"That, in turn, is something I will not query."

"Thank you."

"Shall we begin?"

"What does receipt of your gift entail?"

Grish savagely twisted his finger off. Trails of silver mist drooled from the injury. He reached forward and wiped the stump on each of Droon's red optics.

"Now we shall see if the mist likes you. Or as my Jhangshryn put it: 'considers you worthy'."

Droon sat still. Grish watched the silver tendrils vanish into the cracks and apertures about the eyes. He smiled as the eyes brightened.

"The process of improvement is started."

"Improvement?"

"The mist cannot leave be. It has to *do*. Therefore, if it is not repairing, it is interfering: upgrading its host toward ends my Jhangshryn would never reveal."

Droon raised a finger: "That is why you are never fully healed, isn't it?"

"For you, a millennia of enhancement will be beneficial. After that, I would lose a finger or toe every now and then."

"Noted, Grish Noman. Your favour is paid bar the advent of the rising of your progenitors."

"An event never to occur."

"There are undroids aplenty working in supposed secret to restore their creators. Why not the Jhangshryn?"

"Because I am not beholden."

"For why?"

"I do not recall. The reason is lost. But the imperative remains: I can never be complete."

"Then I shall abide your counsel. Until then, my art calls."

Grish had held his severed finger to the stump while they talked. It was reattached, although it would not be firm for a few days. He bowed as Droon rose and moved slowly to draw his katana, head moving like he was looking about with renewed interest. Neither of them spoke as Grish took his leave.

Through a teeming, humid jungle a predator moves with stealthy ease. Far behind him, two halves of an insect, each with a single wing, spin down onto a marble floor.

GRISH

Serve Cold

The sun is barely up and it's over a hundred degrees out here. The humidity must be low as well, because I'm a dry bird in a wetsuit, with hair that looks like rat-tails and a bad case of saltwater residue chafing - everywhere. I am definitely in the right mood to do bad things.

The ThunderChild pulse gun in my right hand is deceptively light. It can blow holes in things and people like you'd expect from a bazooka. Rather than something that looks like a carbon-fibre short plank.

Onto the deck and the refraction from the windows tells me that they are opaqued for the inside view. Someone likes it dark. I am a contrary bitch this morning, so my opening blast turns the window panel on the dawn side into several kilos of slivers and shrapnel. I'm not blind to the fact that being barefoot means I have just turned the interior of the room into hostile footing. That's not actually a problem. Whatever is in there I have no desire to share air with, let alone the same room.

I hear howls of insult and injury, so I turn myself a few degrees left and blow the wood-panelled wall between window frame and slatted door to splinters and shrapnel. The howls get deeper and the insults turn downright nasty. That's fine, you treacherous bastards, this is going to get real personal.

Dropping my aim, I switch the ThunderChild to automatic and pull the trigger all the way back. It seems wrong that this much destruction can be wrought without recoil – the joy of Delaguen energy weapons technology.

From a movement standpoint, my body looks like it's hosing down a hedge, arm describing leisurely arcs. From an impact standpoint, this damn beach-front residence is being blown to flinders. I have no idea how many furry gangsters my former partner has in there, and there is no way I could take them all in hand-to-claw combat. So gratuitous overkill via building demolition will have to do.

They say that revenge is a dish best served cold.

But they say nothing about consistency.

Purée is good for me.

Forever Song

Whales have long been creatures that inspire awe in humans. When we discovered them out here, that mystery only deepened. At what far distant point, and how, did a star-roving behemoth come to dwell in the oceans of Earth? The xenologists used the Latin word for star to name the new family group, from which the common name, Astruma, came easily.

I've been herding these monstrosities for a decade and even now, they fascinate me, take my breath away and make me feel so small. My ship, the ketch 'Fairtrade', is an old tub, lumbering her thirty metres about on long-obsolete gravitic cores and having to hitch a ride on transluminal haulers to get between herds. The lads in the new cutters, all dash and sleek and barely fifteen metres long, ridicule me at every opportunity - until a herd needs gentling or a bull gets surly. Then Petey Mendez and his rustbucket get to be real popular.

Like now.

I don't know which wag christened the bull of the Epsilon herd 'Moby', but he gave that damn great beast a heritage it seems to be determined to live up to. Like my granddaddy said: "Name things with care, for names bestow as well as limit." Today the five hundred and sixty-seven metres and Lord-knows-what tonnage of Moby has stove in two cutters and cracked a relay station. He's royally peeved at something and no-one wants to go out and play.

"He's coming round the asteroid, Petey. Must be doing nigh-on eighty knots."

I do the conversion in my head while wishing herdsman usage of Earth nautical terms would cease. Astruma use a chronophasic ability to move. It seems rude to measure something about transposing time and space in yocto-increments in such an archaic way.

Oh well, time for the Mendez secret weapon. I cue the audio and let it play. The dichotomy of using such tranquil beauty in the face of such incredible danger is just so Zen to me. I close my eyes and let the sounds take me away.

I paid a fortune for this recording. Captured in the depths of the Mariana Trench, the song of a thirty-two metre female blue whale lasts for a couple of hours. I have a hundred kilowatts of antique valve speakers rigged between the inner and outer hulls. The outer hull of all ketches is high-ferric alloy; they were the last of the deep space ironsides before ceramics, laminates and sleight fields redefined shipbuilding.

No-one has told me why this works. Last time I checked, sound doesn't travel well in vacuum. Then again, Astruma were inconceivable until we found them living out here. Who knows what they can detect? All I know is that I play this recording loud and they seem to like it.

I lie peacefully meditating in the biggest man made sound box to ever grace the void as Moby eases his charge and heaves-to alongside. Before the hour is out, I have the entire three hundred plus herd hanging motionless about me, all exactly aligned to my ships' bearing and all completely tranquil.

As the recording finishes, I open my eyes to see a single ebon eye the diameter of a cutter regarding me through the cockpit veiwports. In that moment, we share something that surpasses all fumbling communication attempts. I see the intelligence behind his eye and he sees whatever he sees in the tiny creature in the metal tube that was filled with noises that reach so far into both our ancestral memories.

Homo Sapiens and *Mysticeti Astrum* stare at each other for a minute or two more, then he blinks and moves off. I watch his glistening hide stutter by.

Ahab would have understood, although I doubt he would have sympathised.

Costs

David's blaster shrieks again and the grey-suited guard flies backwards, chest scorched and bubbling. I repeatedly flick Nancy's katana, but the ichor that looks like blood will not move.

My left foot completes the step I paused so I could shoot steady. I'm not sure how far I've come, but the woodwork seems more like that of a grand residence than ancient, hidden lair. Hopefully, I'm nearly outside.

Captured and contained in the dungeon quarter, where they keep people who've seen through their masquerade, but have no value to the crusade alive or dead. Our destiny was to become ration bars. Apparently when you mulch a human, all you have to do is add a little milk, some semolina and a pinch of salt.

We had no intention of being anything except a nuisance - or, more preferably, a nemesis. It took us twenty-six days to compromise the door mechanisms, and Trudi died to prevent the guard raising the alarm. We put her body on top of Marco's and Sandra's, then lit all three. We may have to leave comrades behind, but none of ours get to be snacks for Gridaerk troops.

From the dungeon quarter to the assembly areas took several hours and cost us Rudin and Vestin, brothers who did everything together – including dying, sadly. The Gridaerk were alerted and threw everything at us. The fact we were inside their headquarters prevented them from using anything we couldn't melee our way through, but what they could use cost us - and them - dearly.

We were an elite unit, somewhere beyond special forces, designed for combating unknown alien threats. Which meant we had to be ready for anything. But the 'anything' we weren't ready for was infiltrators within the armies of mankind.

Gridaerk look like us. Chances are, we share the same brood stock, far back when the Forerunners seeded this universe. But that is as far as similarities go. The Gridaerk are alien within, possessing a minds of extraordinary cunning, high intelligence and, as far as all evidence goes, an unreasoning hatred of humanity.

So here I am, the last 'man' standing in this sorry pile of a wood-panelled fortress. I'm not sure how many of the bastards we killed, but I know I've done for thirty since going solo, using the last of our grenades to make my late comrades unusable. I rarely see Gridaerk, whether through attrition or concealment, I don't know.

But I do know they've got reinforcements coming, and I'm hoping that strategic and suspicious minds will note the undue haste and add that to a file that I fervently hope is being kept, somewhere in Earthforce Intelligence. A file that will tip the balance into them following the sudden departure of personnel from all over the planet, personnel with no obvious reason to rush to a single isolated location. A following that will include serious firepower and deep hostility.

My unit were very, very good. I trained most of them. But I know that when I get outside, I'm going to need a damn sight more than skill, a sword and a sidearm to come out on top of this.

That likelihood being acknowledged; I'm not smiling about this escape. The cost is too high, and if my one gambit fails, the cost for humanity will be higher.

Relix

The surly Rudnik on the left is Ondy. The one on the right is Donbar. She knows that because Donbar is the pretty one. As she backflips to avoid Donbar's attempt to lop off her legs, Ondy's baelsword goes through the space where her head had been. He grins, showing teeth like green daggers. It's not a pretty sight.

Leyshai has no idea why they're still fighting. Their boss is legal bounty, a very bad being. She's a recognised headhunter: one of the people who clears up the criminals that the Pax Galacta can't reach.

Even showing them the docket hadn't helped. Something about 'honouring their commander'. She wouldn't have minded, but fighting them was cutting down on her playtime. With Grish off visiting some undroid guru, she could get into the sorts of mischief that having a damn-near indestructible killing machine as a partner precluded. Nothing wanted to try its luck when Grish guaranteed it would lose.

Another paired lunge. Leyshai leaps up and over, rolling off Ondy's back, flicking a hatchet to rip the inside of his thigh open. He hoots in agony. She's surprised by how mournful a sound it is.

Donbar trumpets. Grabbing Ondy's baelsword, he comes at her, striped blades flailing. Leyshai waits. The tips of the swords whip plumes of sand into the air as they swing. Now she sees the pattern and has the tempo. Without telegraphing even a hint, she rams her right-hand hatchet into the whirring blades. As Donbar is 'passing back' - uncrossing his arms with both blades going over his head - her hatchet momentarily locks an arm against the flat of a blade. Leyshai doesn't let him recover. Her other hatchet embeds itself in his groin.

While Donbar bleeds out, Leyshai disables Ondy's arms, then steps in and just about takes his head off. She'd been about to swing for the top of his head when Grish's advice came to mind: "Rudnik have skulls like ceraplate. You'd need an industrial press to crack them."

She wipes her hatchets on their bodysuits, then sends her weapons into crushspace storage with a thought. Looking about, she sees part of an ornate rifle butt projecting from the dune ahead. Punching the air, she dances over to the buried weapon.

"Your Rudnik are dead, Dricto."

The reply is a grating falsetto: "No-faced bitch!"

Leyshai shakes her head. The problem with thinking weapons is that they eventually get airs and graces. Some even forget what they were designed for: to help their wielders kill. But Dricto is the only one she's come across who created and controlled a criminal empire, using a series of front bosses who just happened to have him as their only weapon.

She summons a bonded flatliner from crushspace.

"Dricto Relix, I'd read you the docket, but neither of us care. So, you're done."

"Undroi-"

The flatliner flashes and smoke emerges from the sand. The bond strip turns from red to blue. Dricto's metamind has been snapshotted at point-of-erasure: proof of end of AI.

Leyshai pulls the ruined weapon from the sand, bats off any loose material, then sends the junked rifle into crushspace. Flatliners are proven, but she still feels better after she drops the physical remains into something hot. Volcanoes or suns being her preference.

Night's Bloom

Professor Hapson called me from my father's house.

"Come quick, lad. Something awful has happened."

Given the urgency and the hour, I paid out for a steam cab and got to Caen Wood Towers swiftly. The ancestral home was visible across the Heath - all lights being on, even those behind the arched windows of the towers.

As I ran from the cab, the butler opened the door. I was surprised to see Hal still at his duty after all my years away.

His voice was filled with concern: "It's you father, sir. Come over quite queer, he has. Shouting something about 'dark alley loom'. We only just managed to stop him setting light to the carpet in the upper hall."

"Good God, Hal. Have you sent for Stephan?"

"Indeed. Doctor Alarames is on his way."

The good Doctor had accompanied father on his trio of grand tours. The first had been more of a whistle-stop reconnaissance, while the second ended early when they nearly froze to death in Tibet. To this day, they stubbornly refuse to divulge what happened to the other members of their party. The third trip had been to South America, where they disappeared into Aztlan with unseemly glee, apparently without a care for the dangers of the locale. They were gone for nearly three years. Their return made headlines across Europe, feting a fortune in relics and writings packed into dozens of crates. But, for all the acclaim, I remember the two of them being curiously subdued while the celebrations swirled about them.

Father was on his bed, held there by restraints fastened to the bedposts. Seeing the wear upon the posts, I looked at Hal in mute question.

"Indeed, sir. Your father has been taken by fits since about a year after his return from the Americas. They have never been as bad as tonight, though. Usually, a few hour's rest is all that is required for him to thrash it through."

I heard another steam cab pull up, pause, and then depart. From the lower hall, a familiar voice hailed us. "Halloo the house! Where are you?"

"In father's bedroom, Uncle Stephan."

Hal called out after me: "Reginald Hapson is in the kitchens, Doctor Alarames. He's preparing victuals for us all."

"Good grief! Was that Daniel who first replied?"

With a laugh, I strode to the head of the stairs: "Yes, Doctor. The Professor called me. What with father being laid out, there was no-one to gainsay him doing so."

Stephan laboured up the stairs, his sparse frame seemingly overtaxed by the small valise he carried. He talked in bursts as he climbed. Not all of it made sense at the time.

"Hapson had the right of it. I got a whiff of the fetid caves as I exited the cab. We have a problem, Danny boy. And if your father is *hors de combat*, it falls to you, his only get, to step forward."

As he arrived on the landing, I shook his hand and stared him in the eye: "All well and good, except that I have no idea what you two brought back from Aztlan."

Stephan grinned, still a damnably infectious thing: "A little north of there, Danny boy. It's old Maya we're dealing with. Gave the Spanish all sorts of hell, did the Lakam Tun. If you think of Picts crossed with Robin Hode's Merrie Men, then add dark magics, you'll be close. It took the Spanish over two centuries to deal with them. In fact, the last pure blood didn't die until 1799. Unfortunately, his granddaughter still had much of the lore. Your father worked his usual charm and bedded her, of course. Then he upped and disappeared into the jungles for the whole of the time the rest of us spent crating up finds. I actually though he was going to miss the boat, but some locals rowed him out just as we weighed anchor."

Father off wenching and stealing artefacts while Stephan held the fort. It was Egypt all over again.

"What did he make off with?"

Stephan waved his free hand in a gesture of ignorance: "All I saw was the ceremonial rug he had them wrapped in. The only time he tried to tell me, I got such a stench of Yaralum that I laid him out with my tankard. Luckily for me, he didn't remember that bit come the following day. In short: I haven't the remotest clue."

"What is 'Yaralum'?"

"The Lakam Tun underworld, Danny boy. Home to a goodly number of divinities and their minions, if hearsay be any guide. I would guess at all manner of other unpleasantness, too. Problem is, no Englishman has taken time to research their patois, let alone decipher their pictograms. We've got no Rosetta Stone, and don't have the time to use it even if we had an equivalent. I fear we're going to have to perform blasphemous acts just to discover the blasphemous act we need to perform to put this right."

Nice of him to include me.

"I'm regretting I asked. So, what particular variety of blasphemy did you have in mind?"

"The kind that leaves Hal and madam Latley locked in here with your father, whilst we three take a learn-it-as-you-cast-it lesson in Lakam Tun necromancy. But first, we need to gather what Mayan relics and trinkets your father hasn't sold, gifted or gambled away. Of course, if he hasn't got some useful bits hidden about, we may as well flee – unless you're minded to give it your all defending the family home."

There wasn't a reply that wouldn't be facile, so I simply nodded and we set to.

An hour later, we stood in the lower hall with a motley assortment of oddities and relics gleaned from father's study and library. Hapson and Alarames were heatedly disagreeing over the contents of a voluminous wood-bound tome. From above, father's wordless, vociferous cries echoed.

While the learned gentlemen argued and father howled, I found myself drawn to a necklace that had slid to lay at one side of the pile. Without conscious decision, I found it in my hands. The warm, elaborate coils cupped a strange, red flower. Its petals felt soft to my touch.

"Tsul, yawat pixan, asab!"

The words flowed from my mouth in a woman's voice. Stephan shouted something that was lost in the thunder that rolled from deep below Caen Wood Towers. I heard my father scream *"Chulha'ki!"*, then everything became still. I even heard birds calling in fright from the woods upon the Heath.

"Good Lord."

Stephan's aghast whisper made me look toward him. Seeing his expression, I twisted myself about to follow his gaze.

She stood on the mosaic that separated lower and upper halls: adorned with gold, elaborately tattooed - and barely clothed. Her headdress fell to brush the floor, under which her hair descended to bestow some cover upon her derriere. A loin cloth barely kept her modesty intact. Her bust was scandalously ornamented with nothing but a pair of enamelled flowers.

"I am come." Her English was heavily accented.

Stephan had arrived beside me: "Welcome, Madame. I am Doctor Stephan Alarames. Let-"

She struck the silver grey circlets on the backs of her hands together. Stephan went down as if poleaxed.

"Quiet, lesser thief."

Her gaze turned to me: "Son of *kisin pek*, am I free to act?"

That was definitely not a flattering term for my father.

"To do what?"

"To stop the *aak'alyoom* blooming."

"Professor?"

Behind me, I heard pages tearing as they were frantically turned.

"Ah-ha! It's the nocturnal flower from which their implacable death god is born into this world."

"We don't want that to happen, do we?"

"Definitely not, lad. Give her permission."

I smiled at the woman: "You are free to act."

She nodded, then spun and raced into the upper hall, headdress billowing. I turned away quickly, to see Hapson staring at the floor, cheeks flaming.

"Comes from a tropical paradise. No need for clothes."

His tone begged my query: "Explaining the cultural mores does not reduce the impact?"

The reply came in a boyish squeak: "Not one whit, lad." He coughed, then continued in his usual voice: "I shall check on your father. Call if you need me."

He headed for the stairs while I headed for the upper hall.

She stood like a statue, head down, arms wide. The circlets on the backs of her hands moved of their own accord. The noise they made was eerie, but the low moans coming from the carpet at her feet were much worse.

"You have *aakä k'ik'el* in your throw."

"What, now?"

"Glyphs of vile blood were graven upon this weave. I smell char. Why was this not burned?"

"Ignorance."

She smiled· "Quick and true, unlike your father."

Only her circlets moved as she wrestled things unseen with powers beyond my understanding. Then came sounds of a struggle from upstairs.

"Stay. That which opposes seeks to distract."

Time passed. Minutes or hours, I did not know. Not a single runnel of sweat marred her countenance, but the very air became heavy with contested intent. Suddenly, three great knocks rang out far below, and the oppressive atmosphere faded away. I felt like a weight had been lifted from me. I was also lathered like I had run up a mountain.

There was a gusting sigh as she let her arms drop: "The bloom is thwarted once again. To be sure, this throw must be burned, along with everything in that offering pile."

She gestured to the heap of things her necklace had slid from.

"Tell the fool who is your father that pretty girls can always find a *u y-ohel k'ay* to work a song of vengeance, and every singing of that song makes the next one worse. One day, a man's lust will reap a harvest that ends the long count."

Whilst unsure of her exact meaning, I decided that my father had just retired from expeditionary work.

"What now?"

"I return to the *U Ka'ani K'uh.*"

"Which is?"

"My mother's house," she tilts her head, as if musing, "which is in your sky, somewhere."

"Who are you?"

"I am Ix'sakkab, and this ritual is done."

With that, right before my eyes, she disappeared. I was left standing alone on a rumpled carpet.

Last night is an example of why I left home in the first place. Even in a world that accepts the existence of technology and supernature, living at Caen Wood Towers was ridiculously dangerous. Now it seems I must become master of the house, simply to ensure my father does not blithely bring down some ancient Armageddon with his frolicking and stealing whilst playing at archaeology.

Walking Home

I'm pointedly ignoring the cat that's been following me. You can never trust felines; you never know which side – or how many – they're working for. Besides, I have no time for distractions - all the tramp mauling and fanatic maiming has finally paid off: I've found the body.

Looking down at the dead man, I see his cufflinks are scratched golden trefoils, the stained shirt was fine cotton and the ragged suit had been expensive. His hands had been exquisitely manicured, too. Now they're defaced with grazes and cuts. But in the left hand, a piece of burgundy cloth is crumpled, clutched tightly, defying even deaths arrival. I have to break fingers to free the cloth and its contents: compressed ashes.

Who had he been? Someone of import, without a doubt. Someone with conviction. Even in dying, he had feinted with his arm to bely the value of what his fist held. As the fight turned into a merciless beating, it would have hampered him. In the end he died badly, keeping that precious handful safe from harm at the expense of increased agony.

'They' always said that the return of one of the messiahs would usher in a new era of wonder. They failed to appreciate that if said messiah arrived in a place where his teachings were not well-known, his presence could be interpreted as something less than a miracle.

Jesus popped back up in a private graveyard in the Ouachita National Forest north of Arkadelphia, Arkansas. The graveyard was the resting place for the martyrs of an Aryan supremacist group called 'The Sons of Thunder'. They combined a blood-and-thunder fundamentalism with a mish-mash of Nazi concepts and modern survivalist doctrine. The end result of a five-and-a-half-foot tall gentleman with a swarthy complexion, dressed in loose white robes, appearing in their graveyard was a 'trespass warning' delivered by a pair of M4 carbines on full-auto. When this failed to knock the apparition down, one of the shooters resorted to his new toy, an M203 under-barrel grenade launcher. By sheer luck, he had an old XM574 white phosphorous grenade loaded. It seems that Christ was bulletproof, but chemical fire had been unanticipated.

Thus ended the second coming. However, pretty well contiguous with the son of god's latest demise, angels appeared to various devoted people and told them where Christ's remains had fallen. Some authorities are still trying to work out why, if they could find believers so easily, did they let the messiah drop into a Neo-Nazi graveyard in Arkansas?

The end result was a couple of hundred people dropping everything and heading for Arkadelphia, AR. The influx did not sit well with the Sons of Thunder, who were frankly sceptical that the son of god could be taken out with 'wily pete'. Fighting ensued. Reinforcements were called. Local and then national military got involved. News spread. The armed forces factionalised. A full-on, multi-sided infantry war kicked off in Ouachita National Forest. Through it all, a small group of the original faithful - escorted and abetted by some 'renegade' Delta members - reached the ashes of the messiah, scooped him up and got the hell out.

Pretty soon, every form of enforcement in the world had members pursuing a hundred or so suspects, each carrying a handful of messiah to some unknown location that had been specified by the angels. The chaos was unbelievable. When the various non-Christian fundamentalists mixed in, the world suffered a 'jihad spasm' of unimaginable proportions. The good news was that all participants fought to the last, viciously, unforgivingly, and without mercy.

As the dust settled, the world looked about at the mess and passed some fierce laws regarding religious involvement in secular affairs, with landslide approval. The Earth is a quieter place since the 'second coming', that's for sure. There are many more empty buildings, too. Which is why it has taken me so damn long to find this particular dead fanatic.

Gazarniel volunteered for this gig, and Him Below liked the fact that a fallen angel so obscure that mortal texts barely mentioned him could be the one to reduce humanity's trust in all divinities so significantly. Gaz was up for it and He gave him leeway to improvise.

The angels appearing to the faithful was an inspired countermove, but Him on High just doesn't have the rapid response infrastructure we have. Shame we can't discover where they were meant to deliver the ashes, or what was supposed to happen. It's a worry, but Him Below will handle it, of that I have no doubt.

I'm just here to collect his ashes. I drop the cloth and its contents into my handbag. Let's go, my brother. It's a long walk home and I can't drink until the ritual is done and you're reconstituted. Handy that fire's your thing. If they'd stoned or drowned you, I wouldn't be able to have a drink with you for a couple of centuries.

Avert

A slow melancholy comes over me as I see how the forest has reclaimed this abandoned fairground. With sunset's approach, the slow movement of light and shade picks out details, making little mysteries for the observer to ponder. A cruciform dagger stabbed into the wooden floor of a carousel, next to a fallen candlestick and a coil of mouldering rope. I sense that someone had nefarious plans thwarted by unexpected developments.

The soft 'whoosh' of a pod landing a short distance behind lets me know my truancy is at an end. I will have to return to being the leader of a division, part of an organisation that, long ago, was charged with a mighty task. It has since become a host which, I fear, has crossed into zealotry and taken me with it.

Soft footfalls approach – Celestine, at a guess.

"It is time, Genairus."

My guess was correct. I look back at her: "We are finished?"

She nods: "The last conurbation has fallen. All sources of toxicity have been neutralised."

Sentences that cover a multitude of horrors.

"Such a pity. They had so much potential." My whispered comment as I stretch is overheard.

"It was wasted potential. We have done them a service." Not a shred of doubt in her voice.

I turn about, my gaze roving over the shades of green: "Hopefully divinities with strong respect-for-nature tenets will prove sufficient."

She places a consoling hand on my shoulder: "You liked them."

With a smile, I look deep into her eyes, hoping she will understand: "I *always* like them. Planetary salvage is a noble cause, but we commit atrocities to implement it."

I can see Celestine does not understand, considering them all to be aberrants. With a sigh, I gesture for her to precede me. I look back for a final time. The dagger catches a ray of sunlight, then is lost amidst verdant shadows.

Dear humanity, you had such potential in your hands, but your adherence to creeds of self-service perpetually denied the utopia you sought. So we have reduced you, in population and technology, to primitive tribes with new gods. In this global pantheon, we are the penalty for you becoming anything that harms this precious green planet that you occupy. Should we return and find you have developed along ecologically damaging lines, there will be no further attempt at salvage: we will annihilate you.

It has taken us fifty of your years to remove the poisons you deposited. If not for the unique shades of green that your vegetation displays, we would not have bothered.

All I can do is hope that the lesson has been learnt.

What You See

"You've got her! Go! Go!"

I haven't. Gee knows it. You can see it in her eyes.

They can only see through my eyes, not read my thoughts. Which is a good thing, because I wouldn't have been allowed within a city block of this place.

Greta Dean, mistress of moguls, finally reached a point where she knew too many secrets. When assassination failed, charges were brought. Several attempts at arrest were made. They failed, but added more charges to her record. Greta went on the run, a chase that everyone thinks will end here, two continents from the city that was her home.

They brought me in because Gee and I grew up together. Broken homes had separated us and sent us on very different, but equally dark, journeys. I'm beholden to one of the men she escorted, and everybody figures that our history will give me the edge, while my mortgaged cybereyes will make me obedient. Being blinded is always a strong argument for obedience.

"What are you waiting for? Get the bitch!"

"In case you hadn't spotted it, that's a sawn-off shotgun she's holding. It may be vintage, but it'll still take my head off."

"We saw. We'll fix you up. Just get her!"

I know what they mean by 'fix'. Cyberzombies are favoured cannon fodder for organised crime and tyrants the world over. One with my innate skillset and size would be worth treble what I owe on my eyes.

I raise my offhand: "Sorry, Gee. The man says I gotta try."

"I know, Vince. Let's get it over with."

Their anticipation comes across as predatory glee: "She's going down. Get the boys ready."

I step forward and the shotgun blast catches me full in the face. I lurch backwards and fall down the short flight of stairs, losing headset and sundry gear along with my eyes and, I suspect, my face. Shock dampers and trauma injectors work their magic and while I may be uglier than usual on the outside, I'm functional here in my personal darkness.

"Vince. You still with me?"

A hand on my shoulder steadies me while the other slips a connector into the jack behind my ear. Suddenly, I can see a red ruin studded with grit and salt crystals. It has my haircut. I can't help it: I twitch, hard.

"Oh shit! Sorry, babe."

"Darlin', I know you only did it to rouse my ass. Now, put my extra eyes on and let's get gone before they guess the plot change."

She slips the vision glasses on me and suddenly, I'm back. Except my traitorous eyes are forever blind.

"Did you get it all?"

Gee smiles: "Two-hundred and sixty-five million, Vince. There's a private shuttle at Stanstead Spaceport, and we are good to go."

Gee and I never lost track of each other. A dead drop in Epping Forest has been our post box since we were ten. Twenty-two years later, the desperate dreams of two poor kids from south of the river are about to come true.

I lead her to the old laundry chute: "There's a crash mat at the bottom, darlin'. Time we appeared to die."

She kisses what's left of my cheek, hitches her skirt up and jumps in feet first. I fire the shotgun at the ceiling, then dive in after her.

Rolling from the crash mat, I hear the sounds of thugs charging into the building above. Gee hands me her phone. I dial the number as she crouches next to me and pulls the crash mat over us.

The explosion is louder than I expected. I feel debris carom off the mat. The roar of the building collapsing is the only thing that makes me sweat. If the basement is not as reinforced as I think, we're going to be squashed like bugs under a boot.

As the noise dies down, I feel Gee relax.

"We're not dead."

I flick the mat back, making eddies in the cloud of settling dust: "True. But not for long, if we're not gone into the sewers before they start scanning for survivors."

"They'll never find our bodies. We died. Edward and Nancy Balham wouldn't be caught dead in this part of town."

"Balham? Nice touch. Okay, missus B, let's not be late for our flight."

She rises to a crouch and gestures toward the barely discernible manhole cover.

"Lead on, Eddie."

"Eddie? That's going to take some getting used to."

"Several decades, hopefully. Now get your cyberbum moving."

"Yes, dear."

"You're going to regret calling me that."

As I crawl past her, I pull my face into an ugly grin: "I doubt it."

"And you can quit doing that, too."

"Yes, dear."

"Bandage your own face, then."

Lizards of the Lost Publishing

www.lothp.co.uk

Julian's first loves were fantasy and magic; the blending of ancient and futuristic. He started writing at school, extended into writing role-playing game scenarios, and thence into bardic storytelling. In 2011 he published his first books, in 2012 he released more (along with the smallest complete role-playing system in the world). He has no intention of stopping this writing lark, and he'd be delighted if you'd care to join him for a tale or two.

Keep an eye on what he's up to at www.lizardsofthehost.co.uk

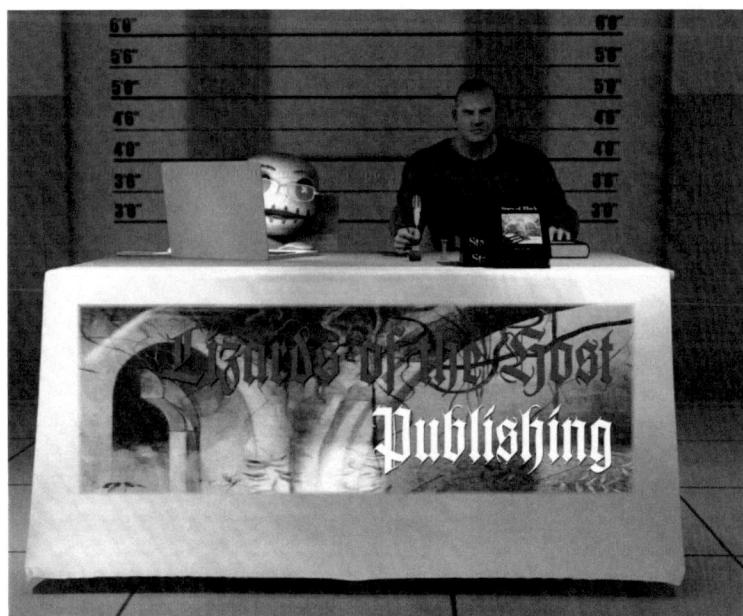

Simon has spent his life wrangling computers, and bears the scars - and skills - to prove it. When he's not programming and/or creating art, he's reading or people watching. He's an aficionado of fine conversation, good coffee and exotic cuisine.

You can see his latest creations at simonjm.deviantart.com

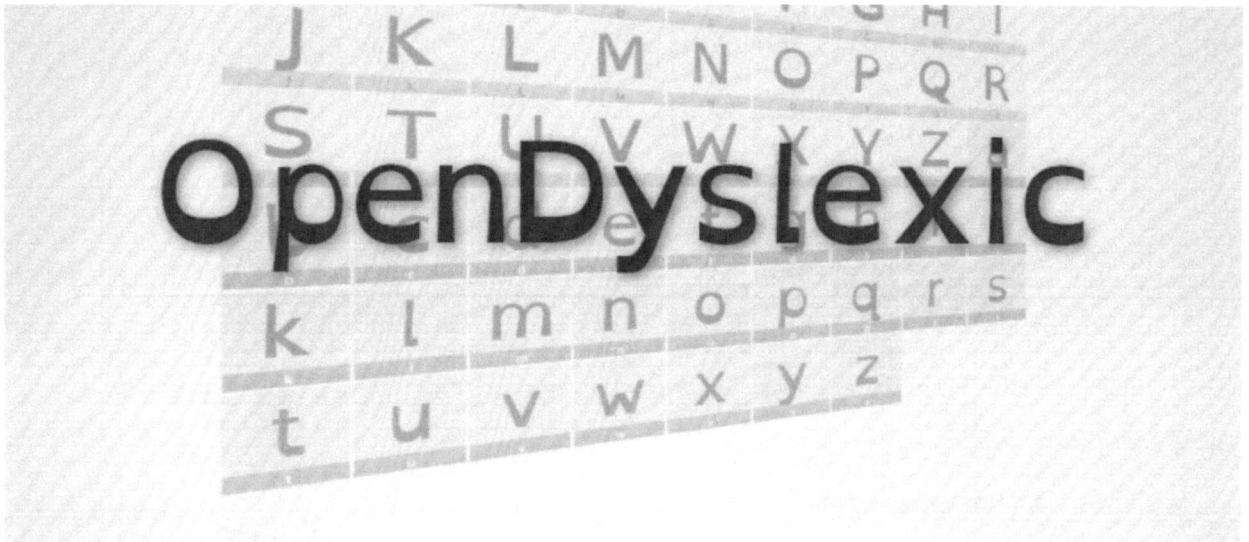

OpenDyslexic is a free font created by Abelardo Gonzalez to help people cope with some of the common symptoms of dyslexia.

Letters have heavy weighted bottoms to indicate direction. You are able to quickly figure out which part of the letter is down, which aids in recognizing the correct letter, and sometimes helps to keep your brain from rotating them around. Consistently weighted bottoms can also help reinforce the line of text. The unique shapes of each letter can help prevent confusion through flipping and swapping.

The OpenDyslexic typeface comes in Regular, Bold, Italic, Bold-Italic and Monospace. The Regular, Bold, Italic, Bold-Italic styles also come in a version with an alternate, rounded 'a'

For more information, please visit opendyslexic.org

This page is printed in OpenDyslexic. This sentence is printed in OpenDyslexic Alta.

I have supported OpenDyslexic since I came across it. Many eBook devices - including Kindle - now offer OpenDyslexic as a selectable font.

With Amazon's Createspace publishing platform able to accept print-ready PDFs (and offering free ISBNs), there is no longer any cost (bar a little of your time) in publishing OpenDyslexic editions of your work alongside the standard editions.

All of my Amazon paperbacks have their equivalent OpenDyslexic editions. Why not join me in working to ensure that how a book is printed presents no barriers to those who want to read?

Thanks and regards,

Julian.

Other Books by Julian M. Miles

The Borsen Incursion, a centuries-spanning space war saga.

ISBN 978-1505781113

OpenDyslexic edition ISBN 978-1519611284

A Place in the Dark, a vampire horror novel. Mature readers only.

ISBN 978-0993287312

OpenDyslexic edition ISBN 978-1530902156

Fire in Mind, a magical and pagan short fiction anthology.

ISBN 978-1511978446

OpenDyslexic edition ISBN 978-1519722171

Stars of Black, a weird horror collection inspired by the original King in Yellow. Mature readers only.

ISBN 978-1511958424

OpenDyslexic edition ISBN 978-1519722720

Single White Male - *An Exercise in Lovecraftian Realisation*, a modern Mythos horror novella. Mature readers only.

ISBN 978-1537157306

OpenDyslexic edition ISBN 978-1537157948

This Mortal Dance, a poetry collection drawn from over thirty years of writing verse.

ISBN 978-1519742858

OpenDyslexic edition ISBN 978-1532804892

The *Visions of the Future* science fantasy flash and short fiction anthologies have been published annually since 2011. The first five are available as paperbacks from Lizards of the Host Publishing (www.lothp.co.uk), while stocks last.

Destinies (2011)	ISBN 978-0957620025
Tangents (2012)	ISBN 978-0957620049
Come Tomorrow (2013)	ISBN 978-0957620056
Agents of Fate (2014)	ISBN 978-0957620087
Infinity (2015)	ISBN 978-0993287305

Alternatively, there are a trio of Amazon exclusive paperback collections that feature three different selections of stories from those first five volumes of the *Visions of Tomorrow* series. Each book also contains two unique tales.

Face Down in Wonderland (2014)	ISBN 978-1503221246
	OpenDyslexic edition ISBN 978-1519722942
Long Way Home (2015)	ISBN 978-1514655863
	OpenDyslexic edition ISBN 978-1519723130
Lifescapes (2016)	ISBN 978-1532740787
	OpenDyslexic edition ISBN 978-1532741159

The sixth volume of the series is available worldwide from Amazon.

Gammafall (2016)	ISBN 978-1535549110
	OpenDyslexic edition ISBN 978-1535562744

Except for *Face Down in Wonderland*, *Long Way Home* and *Lifescapes*, all of these books are available as ebooks from your Kindle store, for Mac and iOS from iTunes, and for all other devices from Smashwords

http://www.smashwords.com/profile/view/JMMiles